JONAH
AND THE
WHALE

GEOFFREY PATTERSON

LOTHROP, LEE & SHEPARD BOOKS · NEW YORK

Jonah lived in a small village in the land of Israel.
He was a lazy man, who spent most of the day lying in
the sun doing nothing while his neighbors worked hard.

The people in the village kept away from Jonah because he was so lazy. This made Jonah unhappy, and at last he asked himself why he found it so difficult to be like them.

Then Jonah heard the voice of God.

"Get up!" said God. He told Jonah to go to the great city of Nineveh and make the people stop their endless fighting with the people of Israel.

But Jonah said to himself, "I can't possibly do that. I am just an ordinary man. Perhaps the people of Nineveh will kill me. I won't go!"

Again he heard the voice of God: "Jonah, you *must* go.
I have chosen you."

    By now Jonah was so frightened that he decided
to run away.

Early the next day he went to the little port
of Joppa. There he boarded a wooden cargo boat
bound for Tarshish, far away from
Israel and Nineveh.

The boat set sail, and soon they were out of sight of land.
Jonah hoped he was out of sight of God, too.

The days and nights passed.

Late one evening the weather grew suddenly stormy.
The sea became a dark, inky black, the waves rose
higher and higher, and the sky turned gray,
the color of granite. The ship was violently
tossed about, tipping the cargo overboard.

Everyone on the boat was afraid and prayed to their gods
to save them from the storm. All except Jonah. He was
fast asleep in the ship's hold.

The others woke him up. "How can you sleep in such
a terrible storm?" they cried. "Who are you?
Why are you here?"

Then Jonah realized that God had made the storm because
he had tried to run away.

"The only way to save yourselves is to throw me into the sea," he said. "Then God will stop the storm."

So reluctantly they took Jonah and threw him over the side into the raging sea.

Instantly the sea became calm.

But Jonah sank slowly down and down, into the darkness. Surely he would drown.

Then out of the blue-black depths appeared an enormous whale many times the size of the ship. With one gulp, it swallowed up little Jonah.

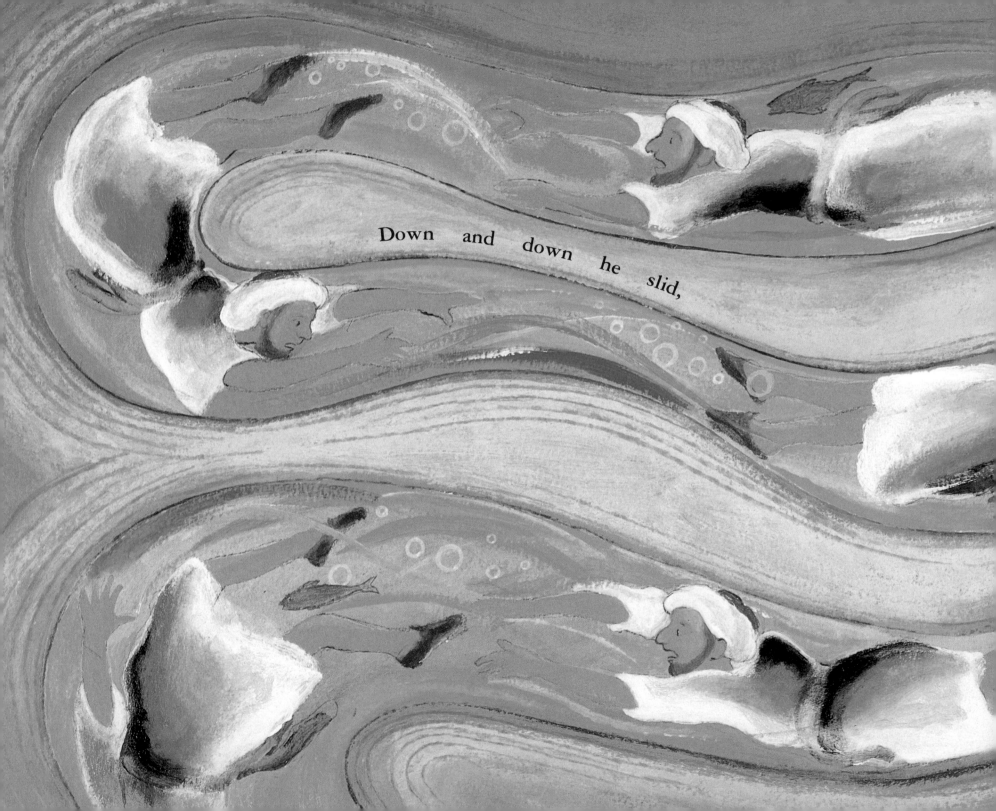

Down and down he slid,

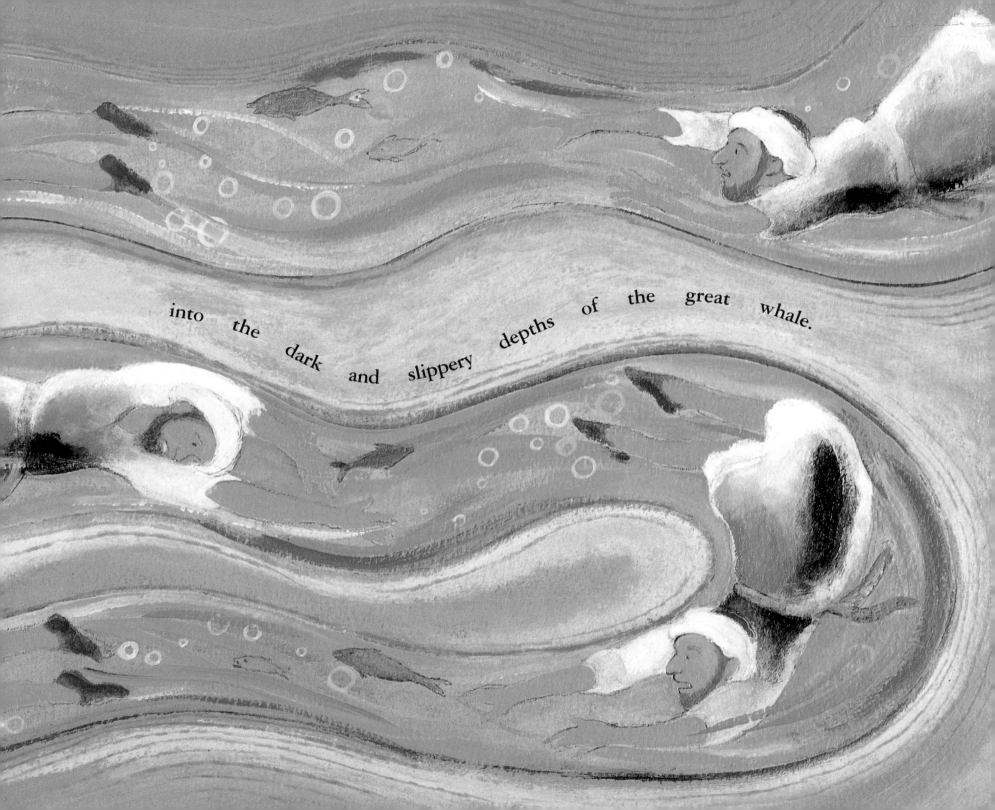

into the dark and slippery depths of the great whale.

At last he came to a stop in the whale's stomach.

It was dark and damp and strange rumbling noises echoed around him.
Poor Jonah sat huddled up for many hours, feeling very sorry for himself.
But then he realized that the whale had saved him from drowning, and he
began to understand that he was inside the whale because he had tried
to run away from God.

Jonah spoke to God from the whale's stomach and said, "I trust you
to look after me, and I will do what you ask."

At that moment a light began to glow inside the giant cavern of the
whale's stomach, and Jonah could look around.

For three days and three nights the mighty whale
plunged through the ocean.

On the morning of the fourth day, Jonah felt
the inside of the whale heave and shake like an earthquake.
   Jonah was terrified. "What's happening?" he cried.
   Then he was thrown up in the air, and with a gurgle and
a whoosh, he was pushed and squeezed along a dark slippery tunnel.
Suddenly he saw daylight. The whale's great mouth had opened.

A moment later Jonah was spewed out of the whale and onto the shore!

He knelt beside the sea, raised his hands to God, and thanked Him for saving his life. "Now I will go to Nineveh and give them your message," he said.

The great whale looked at Jonah for a long moment, and then it slowly sank back into the sea.

For Bonny

Copyright © 1991 by Geoffrey Patterson
First published in Great Britain in 1991 by Frances Lincoln Limited, Apollo Works, 5 Charlton Kings Road, London NW5 2SB
All rights reserved. No part of this book may be reproduced or utilized in any form or by any means, electronic or
mechanical, including photocopying and recording, or by any information storage and retrieval system, without
permission in writing from the Publisher. Inquiries should be addressed to Lothrop, Lee & Shepard Books, a
division of William Morrow & Company, Inc., 1350 Avenue of the Americas, New York, New York 10019.
Printed in Hong Kong

First U.S. Edition 1992   1 2 3 4 5 6 7 8 9 10

Library of Congress Cataloging in Publication data was not available in time for publication of this book, but can
be obtained from the Library of Congress, ISBN 0-688-11238-2   ISBN 0-688-11239-0 (lib. bdg.)
L.C. Number 91-53021